HITMAN'S PLUS SIZE LITTLE

Age Play DDlg Romance

Amanda King

ISBN: 9798837441011
Imprint: Independently published

1st edition

Cover design by: Amanda King

CONTENTS

CHAPTER 1

Silvia

I opened my eyes and found myself in a dark room. It was like there was this presence around me, making my existence unbearable. I tried to make sense of everything happening around me, but that was more difficult said than done.

After all, I couldn't remember, anymore, exactly everything that happened after I met up with my uncle at the restaurant. He said something about needing money, and it didn't make much sense.

When it came to money, I didn't have much of it - not in my bank account or with me in my old apartment. And thinking about my apartment, the first thing that came to my mind was my bedroom, which was also my playroom.

But I shouldn't be thinking about it, especially when I had more pressing matters at hand.

Thinking about my hands, though, I noticed that I couldn't move them freely. I felt something a little rash and rough rubbing and scratching on the skin of my wrists, and I knew that it was a length of rope.

My heart rate started to pick up. Where I was, it was dark, but there was a single light bulb hanging from the ceiling. It was high up and I wouldn't be able to reach it with my hands even if I was standing.

There was one more thing about this that I noticed, too. *I wasn't standing.* I was actually lying on the floor, and it was dark and sticky with something. I was hoping that that was thanks to some wetness or water that formed on it, but I couldn't know for sure.

I blinked. I was so anxious and afraid that I almost forgot I could blink. Blinking was good. It allowed me to think better about what was happening and remember what I was doing at the restaurant with my uncle.

He was a drug addict, I remembered, noticing that he was standing on the other side of the room, looking outside as though he was waiting for someone to come. If someone was going to come here, I couldn't know that for sure, but I sure as hell was hoping that nobody was.

In the meantime, I was trying to move my hands, my arms, and also the rest of my body so that I could free myself from the length of rope that kept my hands tied. But whoever had tied my hands with the rope, they did so well – to the point where I was only hurting myself doing this.

"Alphonso, what are you doing?" I murmured, noticing that my voice was so feeble right now that even though everything was quiet around me, I was certain he didn't hear anything.

So much so that I knew it was pointless.

I began to feel this overwhelming sense of loneliness, something that was actually common to me. I always felt lonely, especially because I didn't have anyone I could call my boyfriend or even my Daddy.

Just thinking about that, reflecting on where I lived, I couldn't help but imagine a future where I didn't have anyone.

I would never even lose my virginity, though that didn't matter at all right now.

A second later, I started to hear footsteps coming here. I just realized that I was in a warehouse and that it was massive. It had some old equipment, boxes, and a couple of other industry items I couldn't name, but which were showing their age and that they were covered by a thick layer of dust.

Then, shadows started to emerge behind the open entrance

of the warehouse. I didn't know who they were, but they looked menacing and scary. I felt shivers running down my spine, something that snapped me to this reality where I could die.

"Is she really there?" The man that was leading the group asked, this time finally stepping inside the warehouse. Even though I was still lying on the floor, my hands and my feet tied by lengths of rope, I could tell that he was massive.

He was much more than that, actually. He was tall, well-built, with a square and strong jawline, his eyes intense and focused, and his hair so neat that I couldn't spot a single stray follicle. Just looking at him was making me forget about everything else that was happening here.

"Yes, she is here. I got her here for you," my uncle replied, making me feel rage all of a sudden. My blood started to boil.

I was beginning to wrap my head around what was going on here. He was going to give me to that business-looking man, and I didn't even know why. Unless he was selling me to him, which was a possibility, there was nothing else that could explain this chain of events.

The man standing in front of him looked at me, his eyes growing darker and more menacing. I had no idea who he was, but he couldn't be a normal, upstanding citizen.

The kind of plans he was preparing in his mind right now would make anyone afraid of him.

"Good," he murmured, walking past my uncle without giving him as much as a glance. I wondered why his behavior was like that. If this was a business transaction where my uncle was selling me to the leader of the group, then he should be giving him the money right about now.

And yet, the leader of the group was still marching toward me without showing as much as a hint that he was going to do so. That was why my uncle had this stupefied look on his face, his hands going up and opening, his fingers shaking, and everything else about his body showing that he was as confused as I was.

I couldn't help but chuckle slightly, noticing that the sound that came out of my mouth was so low that not even their leader heard it.

"Wait, are you going to pay me or not? I did everything I could," Alphonso mumbled, but if he thought that his words were going to help things, then he was going to get disappointed.

"Should I really do that, especially to someone willing to sell his own niece?" He asked after stopping slowly and carefully, almost showing that he didn't like that inopportune question at all and was doing everything in his power not to kill him right now, even though he could. That small bump under his suit... It showed that he had a pistol with him and that he wasn't afraid of using it.

"But..." Alphonso mumbled again, but then trailed off, his voice becoming nothing more than a whisper.

"There's no 'but.' You're going to come with us and that's it. Then, I'll think about paying you, though I have to say... it's good that you didn't fail," he said, turning his head so that he was looking at me, and I felt shivers running down my spine when he focused just on me.

It was like there was nothing else around us and that I was the only thing that could ever interest him.

He finished stepping toward me and I noticed his eyes softening up again. Did I think that he was someone with good intentions? Not at all, but he could be my only hope.

Maybe he had some good in his heart, but I wasn't holding my breath for that.

And the fact that I couldn't speak normally? It was because there was some duct tape on my mouth, and it sealed my lips shut.

I couldn't even scream, even though everything in my body was telling me to do so.

He squatted so that he could see me better.

"Tell me, did that man hurt you?" He asked, settling his hand on my shoulder and brushing it slowly and carefully. I didn't like the touch of his hand there and even though I wore a shirt, I could feel the coldness of his fingers seeping into my bones.

I had no idea what I could even say to make him do something else. Whatever he was hoping my answer was going to be, I doubted that he even cared about it.

He took a long, audible breath and then he put his hands under me, under my back and knees, and I knew that he was going to lift me. He smiled softly and his smile faded the moment I heard gunshots in the distance. Men outside were screaming.

I would be screaming right now too if I could, but the duct tape kept my lips sealed, and I was also certain that, if I could do that, it would only make things worse.

After all, the stranger just dropped me on the floor, ran outside holding his gun, and I knew that he wasn't going to stop until the attackers were killed.

"I don't know who's attacking us, but they are going to regret it."

CHAPTER 2

Curzio

I didn't think that I was going to be here, at this warehouse, holding my gun and hoping that I would finally find him. The man that I wanted to see dead more than anyone else, and who was the same person that inflicted so much pain in my life that I wanted nothing more than the double of that in return, his life burning to a crisp and him finally saying that he regretted it all, only to then hear, from my mouth, that I would never forgive him.

His name was Ausilio and he was a bastard that thought so highly of himself, thinking that he was the most important person in the world.

Bullets flew everywhere and some of them even whizzed past me, but for now, I was fine. I was hiding behind the wall and every so often I would peek to the side, trying to see and find out what was happening inside the warehouse.

I asked my men to create some sort of diversion outside, and it appeared to be working. My heart was calm and my grip on the gun was certain. Nothing could make me feel more certain about this.

A diversion, though? It was actually much more than that. I came here with overwhelming force, something I was sure Ausilio was trying to wrap his head around. After all, he never thought that I was going to track him down. It wasn't easy, but my plan worked in the end, and now I could finally have his life… if it wasn't for something that was holding me back and making me change my plans.

I knew that Ausilio was outside and shooting at my men. I could rush over there and meet him face-to-face, but there was something - or rather someone - lying on the floor of the house, and I wasn't a monster that was going to leave her alone and fend for herself.

Even though I could only see her behind, peeking every so often, I knew she was young and, quite frankly, stunning.

She was the sole reason why I wasn't heading in the other direction after hearing Ausilio's voice as he boomed his commands. The only thing I was hoping for right now was that none of my men was going to be killed, despite the unlikelihood of that.

I decided to turn my body and enter the warehouse. Everyone else was outside, shooting and trying to kill each other.

I felt calm, heading to the struggling woman on the floor. She must've heard my footsteps, for she rolled over as swiftly as she could, her eyes finding me only a couple of moments later.

She gasped after noticing my pistol and that I was pointing it at her. It wasn't my intention to be doing that, so I corrected it in a heartbeat, but I didn't put my gun back under the waistband of my pants. Rather, I kept it low and pointed to the floor instead.

I looked at the floor, noticing how dusty and wet it was. It was another reason why I thought this woman shouldn't have been left lying on the floor like this, staring at me with such wide eyes I wondered what was going on in her mind at the moment.

She couldn't speak, I thought after noticing the duct tape on her mouth.

"I'm going to free you. Don't worry," I announced, taking out my military-grade knife and slicing and cutting the ropes that tied her wrists and ankles together, freeing her, but not entirely.

There was still the duct tape on her mouth, which I peeled off.

Then, she stood up slowly and when she tried to run away from me, she lost her balance. She was going to fall over face-first on the floor, but I grabbed her wrist and held her strongly, not hurting her.

After she regained her balance, I said, "As I said before, I don't know who you are, but don't worry about it. I'm not here to hurt you."

"But who are you?" She asked as she raised her voice, something I didn't want to happen. Without thinking twice about it, I just clamped my hand on her mouth, stopping her from making another mistake. I just didn't want Ausilio to find out that I was here and had her. Not right now, anyway, imagining that he was going to come to that conclusion soon.

"That doesn't matter right now," I affirmed, checking my surroundings and thinking. It was likely that I was going to find Ausilio again, though I couldn't even begin to imagine when.

This woman right here, whose name I didn't know, needed to be helped. This warehouse was located on the outskirts of the city and there were no cars nearby and no one that could take her somewhere safe. She was relying on me right now to survive this, something that made me bite my bottom lip in frustration.

It took me so long to track down Ausilio, and I never thought that a woman, probably in her twenties, was going to stop me from having my revenge.

And yet, I just didn't see another way out of this.

"How come it doesn't?" She asked, trying to make herself look tougher than she was, but it didn't work.

I had to make a decision and I made it, taking her outside with me as fast as our legs could move. When we were outside, I could still hear the sound of the guns firing, meaning I had to end this before it was too late.

After all, at this point, it was likely that Ausilio and some of his men had run away. It was just the way he was. He tried to look tougher than he was, but in the end, he was nothing more than a cockroach. An annoying, pesky cockroach, but still nothing more than that.

I sent a message to my second-in-command, calling off the attack and stopping it. Right on cue, I thought, as everyone stopped shooting and everything appeared to be calming down.

I noticed that the woman whose arm I was still holding was shaking slightly. Her arm was trembling, something I didn't like to see. I was a Daddy. I wasn't going – and I would never – tell her that, but I was.

And if there was something I didn't like seeing, it was a beautiful woman like her going through so much and suffering as much as she was at the moment.

"Looks like the fight is over. I know who kidnapped you and who was after you. I'm going to kill him and the rest of his gang," I promised, noticing that she was looking at me with concerned eyes.

She was most likely wondering what the hell even happened here. But it was pretty simple. Since I knew that Ausilio was going to be here, I made sure I came to this place with overwhelming force. And it was enough to destroy most of his men and make him think twice before showing up anywhere again.

I didn't do this often, though. Even though I was the leader of the Fiorentini family, I preferred to act in the shadows and lead my men from behind. But this was different, especially when it came to Ausilio.

I couldn't help but feel my blood boiling, thinking about all the things he did to me, all the people he killed, and pretty much everything else that reminded me of his existence.

She looked up and I asked, "What's your name?"

"It's... Silvia," she responded and I knew that it took everything she had to say that. So much so that it wasn't surprising when she then threw her arms around me. She pressed her body tightly against me, and I could feel how warm she was.

She started to sob and cry, and also whimper, and I couldn't help but tuck my gun in my waistband so that I could do something I didn't think I would.

Silvia... It was a beautiful name and one I would never forget.

I was tall enough to put my chin on her head, my hands moving slowly over her back to comfort her. And it worked, her sobs and her crying died a couple of minutes later.

When she was feeling better, she pushed herself away from me and wiped the tears from her eyes. "I'm sorry, I didn't mean to hug you like this."

"I think that first I need to introduce myself. I'm Curzio. Curzio Pugliesi and I lead the Fiorentini family. It's not something that I thought I would do, but since Adelmo decided that he didn't want it anymore, it's up to me now to make sure that I can finally kill the person that was going to 'buy you.'"

And just mentioning that term was enough to make my stomach churn.

She was a person like everyone else, and also much more than that. Even though I didn't know her well, I could tell that she seemed to have a good heart.

"Well, it's good to know you and I'm so happy that you saved me, but I don't think I can stay here long. I need to go back to my life, to my work, to my studies, and pretty much everything else."

And the moment she said that, I just couldn't help myself. I had to make a request that I had no idea if she was going to accept or not. After all, she didn't know that I was much better than the person that was going to buy her.

She thought, given the shootout and everything that happened here at this warehouse, that I was just as dangerous.

"Do you want to go with me to my house? I don't think you can go anywhere from here without a car and there's none nearby."

CHAPTER 3

Silvia

I knew he was thinking about inviting me somewhere, but I didn't think it was going to be at his house. But calling it a house was short-selling it. It was so much more than that. From the outside, it was massive, the kind of work whose artists and engineers probably felt proud of it just thinking about it.

Even while I was still seated inside his black sedan, the mansion overwhelmed me. I could imagine myself living for months – if not years - there, even though I knew that it would never happen.

I was just stepping out of the car after he opened the door for me, thinking that this was nothing more than a temporary solution. Once I was back on my feet, I would make sure that I had enough money to get by.

In the meantime, I was thinking about how I was going to tell the police about my kidnapping. They would have so many questions, including about the involvement of this man that was helping me.

I just finished getting out of the car when I realized that he was holding out his hand for me. I never thought he would be doing something like that, and it made me feel a little ashamed of myself.

And yet, I still took his hand and he led me inside the mansion, up the steps in the main hall, and then he stopped in front of a room. We remained there for a couple of seconds, nothing happening around us.

I felt so small in his presence. He was massive, standing in front of me and his eyes checking me out from bottom to top. Even though most other women would be thinking that there was something wrong with his intentions, I was thinking the opposite.

Just checking out his gaze was enough to tell me he had no ill intentions toward me.

"This is your room," he announced, putting his fingers around the doorknob and turning it.

I padded inside carefully and with utmost attention as the door opened, revealing one of the most jaw-dropping rooms I had seen in my life. It was so much more than my old bedroom in my apartment, if it could even be called that.

I took a couple more steps inside the bedroom and found myself surrounded by so many items I had never seen in my life. Even the bed was different, more luxurious, and fancier, and the mattress was the kind of thing where I could imagine myself lying on it for hours on end, not doing anything important or stressful.

Curzio was behind me when he asked, "So, do you like it?"

In the meantime, I couldn't help but wonder what he did for a living if he had so much money and power. After all, looking outside, I couldn't help but notice the jaw-dropping number of men walking around the property, patrolling the perimeter.

It was more than obvious that he was no common businessman. He was so much more than that, making me have so many questions about his past and his current life.

"Yes, it's amazing. I'm so happy that you are letting me live here for now," I replied after clasping a hand on top of the other, putting them both against my belly as if I was protecting myself.

Right now, he didn't look like my savior at all. I didn't know his name, but one day I would. I had to if I wanted to see him behind bars.

"Well, I'm glad that you do," he said, coming with me to one of the doors of the room. I didn't know where it led, but I had a hunch, and it was the right one when he opened the door, I noticed.

It was the closet and it had almost everything I could ever want. More clothes than I could ever imagine myself wearing one day, shoes, accessories, and everything else. Everything else except a collection of tiaras, Disney shoes, cute and childish bracelets, and a catalog of dresses so that I could look like Snow White.

He turned his head slowly, his eyes looking at me filled with kindness. "And what do you think about this closet? Good enough for you?"

Why was he even asking me that question? I asked myself, stepping inside the closet with him and realizing that it was bigger than my old bedroom in my apartment. Remembering it, I knew that I wasn't going to be going back there anytime soon.

I mumbled, "I don't even know what to say. You have this house that looks more like a mansion and you were keeping this room looking tidy for someone like me to come and live here?"

It was an appropriate question to ask right now. After all, who was he, and what was he hiding from me? The more time passed and the more he showed me about his life, the more I learned that he was anything but a run-of-the-mill businessman.

He turned his head around slowly and carefully, his eyes checking every part of the closet. With his hands inside his pockets, he responded, "This was actually going to be for someone else, but things didn't work out between us."

Did he mean that he was thinking about me the same way? That I was going to become his girlfriend or something like that? I didn't know, but it was a possibility, one that made me feel jitters in my stomach, something that didn't happen often.

"Not that I think anything is going to happen between us, mind you. I was just answering your question," he added to his initial response and something in the closet caught my attention all of a sudden, and I ran up to it in a heartbeat.

It was a small, childish but made with high-quality materials tiara, and I couldn't help but put it on my head right at that moment, letting my Little side come out. It was something that happened naturally and that I was unable to control until I realized it was already too late.

When I realized that, I blushed. The first thing that came to my mind was that Curzio was going to throw me out of the mansion. And if he did that, I would be devastated.

Either that or the chances of me becoming his girlfriend were going to be thrown out the window.

I ripped the tiara off my head, putting it back where I found it. "I'm sorry. It's just that I really like childish stuff, and this tiara is so beautiful."

A moment of silence hung in the air and I couldn't help but wonder what was going on in his mind. Seconds later, Curzio waved his hand up and down, dismissing my words.

"Don't worry about it. It's just something that was left here by my previous partner. I forgot that I should get rid of it."

Another moment of silence and I didn't know what to say. He was being so kind to me, inviting me to live here with him, and I couldn't just throw him several questions that would make him concerned about his decision.

We stepped outside the bedroom and then he closed it, but gave me the key for it. I held it in my hand, checking it carefully and pressing my fingers on it as if it would fade away if I wasn't doing that.

His voice boomed in front of me, snapping me back to the reality that surrounded me.

"We are also about to have dinner. Do you want to eat? I would understand if you don't," he asked, turning his body slightly so that his invitation was more alluring and his chances of convincing me were better. He didn't need to be doing that, though.

My stomach was rumbling. I wanted to eat something and if the food was good, then I would eat much more than just 'something.'

CHAPTER 4

Curzio

I could put the stuff about killing Ausilio on the sidelines, for now, I thought, walking around the table and sitting down across from Silvia. She was seated at the table and her eyes were going from side to side, checking every option she could have for dinner.

A moment of silence as the waiters and the waitresses continued to add more food options on the table. Our dinner could make anyone's mouth water. Kobe beef, lobster, one-pan creamy chicken, and pretty much everything else one could imagine.

And yet, Silvia wasn't moving her hands yet, something that troubled me slightly.

I lifted my hands, saying, "You can choose anything you want. I've asked my cooks to prepare this for you." And I did that right after I knew we were going to come here together. I wanted to give my cooks enough time to prepare the food, and it looked like it worked.

The food was delicious. The smell was strong, filling my lungs. I couldn't have asked for a better dinner.

And yet, it was also just for the two of us. Once the waiters and the waitresses left, we would be alone. I wasn't thinking about doing anything to her she didn't want, of course. For now, I was just happy seeing her smiling. I figured that it wasn't something she did often.

"But there's just so many," she confessed and the right words came to my mind.

"Well, in that case, I can choose the food for you," I said after pointing with my index finger at some of the options on the table. They were simple but healthy options, and she was going to enjoy eating them.

That was my Daddy side coming out and exposing itself.

Silvia looked like a Little that needed some guidance and I was more than willing to provide it for her.

My eyes looked determined and confident as well about my decisions.

"In that case, then, I suppose I have no option but to pick what you've chosen for me," she responded, and just when she was going to take from the first platter on the table, I held up my hand and opened it, making a stop sign.

"Actually, let me do this for you," I said, standing up and going around the long table until I was behind her. When I was, I filled her plate with all the food options that I wanted her to eat.

I wanted her to be healthy and to only eat the best, so I didn't go overboard with my choices.

"Wow," she said, her voice suddenly much more childlike. This was so conflicting. Everything about her showed me that she was a Little, and yet everything else also pointed out that she wasn't. I just didn't want to come across as a weirdo if I asked her that question and she said she didn't know anything about Daddy/ Little dynamics.

"It's all for you, and I hope you like the food," I said, and then I went back to where I was sitting before, digging into the food after filling my plate.

Some minutes later, when our bellies were already a little full and Silvia was better used to this environment, I found her eyes again, and then I decided to ask, "Do you know anything about the person that was going to 'buy' you?"

Her hand stopped where it was and before she could eat the piece of steak that was on the fork, she put it down slowly and I noticed that her hand was shaking slightly.

My question was necessary. There were so many things about Silvia I wanted to know. One of the things about Ausilio was that he never did anything without a good reason. If he wanted Silvia, then it was for a good reason, and he certainly didn't want just another toy.

"I don't know anything about- what was his name again?" She asked, her voice lacking her initial joy, something that hurt me a little.

"It's Ausilio. He's Italian, like me," I responded and she gulped, picking up the glass with orange juice and then chugging down some of it.

She put it down and replied, "Well, I don't know anything about him, but I know a lot about my uncle. I don't know what I was thinking, going to the restaurant with him and hoping that he was going to turn things around for his life. He was the one that kidnapped me and put me in that warehouse."

My hand went for my wine glass and I lifted it, taking a sip. "Your uncle?" I asked, hoping that I wasn't prodding a topic even more sensitive than the one we were already talking about.

She nodded once and slowly, looking down as if she was feeling shame. I noticed the twinkle of a tear coming out of her right eye, and I reached over the table, put my hand under her chin, and I lifted it slightly.

"Don't worry about him or anyone else, for that matter. Just let it all out and tell me everything you know."

"His name is Alphonso Ragusa and he's always been problematic. He's addicted to heroin, and I think that he was going to sell me to Ausilio so he could make some money. I see now that he's willing to do anything to continue his addiction."

Her saying that made me tighten up my grip on the glass of wine on the table. My knuckles were white.

"I don't know what you were thinking, meeting up with him alone at a restaurant, but if I was there, I wouldn't have let you," I replied after considering my words carefully.

She looked up after I pulled my body back and retreated my hand. What I did – lifting her head slightly with my hand – helped her feel better, but I didn't want it to become weird.

"Thank you. I think that I most likely need someone like you in my life," she said and it made me wonder again about the possibility of her being a Little. I still wasn't going to bring that up, and yet my mind couldn't help but start to obsess over it.

Minutes later, we finally finished eating dinner, and then we stood up. I guided her out of the dining room and took her to the top of the staircase in the main hall, from where she was going to her bedroom. Her bedroom was on the right side and mine was on the left one. I wanted Silvia to feel she had enough space to be able to think about everything that happened.

She stood in front of me with her hands covering the lower part of her belly. She looked so innocent with her head tilted down, staring at the floor.

"I want you to know that you are going to be safe here with me, but if you don't mind," I said and she tilted her head up, finding my eyes. Tears formed a gentle layer on her eyes. "If you could tell me something else about your uncle, maybe where he likes to hang out, then maybe we could solve this sooner than we would without that information."

"Well, there's this place where he goes often. It's pretty sketchy, though. It's a dive bar located at..." She started to say as she gave me the address of the place. It was indeed pretty sketchy, I thought, looking it up on Google Maps. So much so that anyone who didn't know anything about the place would probably overlook it when walking past it. But for me, it was different.

Considering that it was a place where he liked to hang out often, then it was a place of extreme importance to me. Finding out her uncle meant sniffing out Ausilio too, and that thought alone was enough to motivate me.

"Thank you for this information, Silvia. It's extremely useful to me," I said and then added, "and I hope you have a good night's sleep. If you don't, you can ask one of the butlers for sleep medicine. We have a few here."

"Thank you. You are really so kind," she said and I nodded before turning around slowly, and then when I was going to my bedroom – it was a tiresome day and I just wanted to get some sleep – she grabbed my hand. Her hand was incredibly tiny compared to mine.

She was staring into my eyes with determination as she said, "Could you please not hurt my uncle? I know that he kidnapped me, and that's something I will never forgive him for, but he's still family and I just want to know that he's going to be okay."

She was asking that of me? I was conflicted, but since I knew how good her heart was, then there was no helping it. Not to mention that she was the kind of person that I would never do anything that could hurt her, that request included.

I took a long breath and then promised, "Alright. I'm not going to hurt him."

CHAPTER 5

Silvia

I woke up and found myself lying in the bed, gazing at the ceiling and unable to stop thinking about everything that happened so far. I couldn't stop thinking about Curzio, how good he was to me, how sweet he was when he wanted to be, and pretty much everything else about him.

I just never thought I would meet someone that treated me with such respect.

That was one of the reasons why I couldn't sleep. I tossed and turned in the bed, thinking that I was going to eventually fall asleep, but it didn't happen. In the meantime, something I never thought would happen was. I was starting to hate the bed.

Without thinking twice about it, I slid off the bed, slipped my feet into a pair of loafers, and then padded over to the balcony. My eyes turned left and right and I checked the beautiful, stunning garden that the balcony overlooked.

Even though it was dark and everything around me was so quiet I could even hear my own breathing, I suddenly found myself wishing to go down there, to the garden, to explore it for a little while, but I knew that I couldn't.

Someone like Curzio, living in this kind of place and surrounded by guards as tough-looking as the ones I was seeing, really couldn't be anyone that I should draw any attention from, I thought.

Then, I started to remember my uncle and everything that happened before I ended up here. I began to remember everything he told me, that we were going to start living together, that he was going to start a new job in a better place, and that everything was going to be much better.

But then, he drugged me, took me to that warehouse, and tried to sell me to Ausilio. Just thinking about that, my stomach churned.

And that coupled with all the shit going on in my life, I couldn't help but start to cry. It happened almost as something innocent that I was going to be able to control and hold back, but then I learned how wrong I was. The tears started to come out, rolling down my cheeks, and I had to move away from the balcony as fast as possible.

If there was something I learned living this shitty life I had, it was that I couldn't let anyone see my weaknesses.

I was almost in the middle of the bedroom when I heard someone walking past the door. I tried to stop crying at that moment, but it was too late. The moment that the person heard me crying, he stopped, making me wonder if he was just one of the guards or someone else… or even Curzio himself.

I tilted my head up slightly when I heard his voice coming from the other side of the door, sneaking through the gaps.

"Silvia, is everything okay with you?" He asked, taking a couple more steps until he was closer to the door. I wondered if I should even reply or if I should pretend that I didn't hear him.

But then I realized that doing something like that was actually stupid. He lived here and I was certain that he knew everything about this mansion, including that the door gaps were large enough to let sounds through them.

"Everything's fine with me, Curzio, but… Thanks for asking," I replied after taking a couple of steps to the door. Then, I slowly put my fingers around the doorknob and tried to turn it. A moment later, I realized that I was possibly making one of the biggest mistakes of my life.

What if he were to take advantage of this moment and do

something to me that I didn't even want to think about? I asked myself, realizing that the possibility of that happening was actually pretty high.

After all, I didn't know much about Curzio and what he was like – what he was really like, especially when he was feeling that nobody would ever find out about what he did.

But what I was thinking was still not fair to him, thus I still opened the door, albeit slowly and carefully. In case he tried anything, I'd shut the door in his face, jump out the window, and run away from here as quickly as I could. He wouldn't be able to do anything… Except for the fact that the walls of the mansion were so tall that I wouldn't be able to climb over them. Everything I was thinking right now felt so stupid.

"Hi," I said lowly and weakly, supporting my weight against the doorway.

His eyes checked my face carefully, reminding me that I didn't even remember to wipe the tears on my face. I should've done that so that he didn't find out I was really crying and had just lied to him about it.

"You're really crying. Why?" He asked, and even though there was a hint that he asked me that question because he was genuinely worried about me, I knew that his reasons were deeper than that.

Curzio wasn't just worried about me – he wanted to know everything about me. I supposed that was his dangerous, hidden side – the one that he wasn't keen on talking about – speaking louder right now.

This was his house and I had to obey him, especially because I was always so submissive. That was my Little side speaking louder than the right thing I should be doing right now.

I finished opening the door, noticing that his pajamas made him look even more stunning than normal. I couldn't help but scrutinize every little detail of his body, which in turn made me feel tingles in my pussy.

I knew that thinking that way about this was wrong. After all, Curzio was my host and so far he had been doing everything right for me, including letting me sleep in this spacious, fancy room.

I sat down with him on my bed and without warning me, he put his arm around my lower back, and he didn't pull me to him like I thought he was going to. Instead, he just kept it there, his eyes studying my expression to make sure that I wasn't going to scream or do something worse.

His arm around me actually made me feel safer. I loved it. There was something about the warmth coming from his body that I couldn't put into words.

"Now you can tell me about what's troubling you," he said and I just had to let everything out. Every little thing, even the fact that I was a Little.

When that part came out, I feared he was going to start shooting several questions in my direction, but he didn't. He was still just looking at me, studying my behavior.

When I was done, I was huffing slightly. Everything I said took a toll on me, and I wasn't going to hide that.

"I'm sorry I had to vent like that," I said, trying to stand up and move away from his arm, but I knew that it was pointless.

Curzio was holding me to him without intending to be doing that, and I was letting him. Tears coming out, I couldn't help but feel drawn to him, his lips approaching mine, everything going still around me, and then we... kissed.

His lips were remarkably soft and tender, and I couldn't stop kissing him. It was the first time that I was kissing someone, but of course I wasn't going to tell him that. I didn't want him to think, while we were kissing, that he was doing so with someone so inexperienced.

We weren't using our tongues – not yet, anyway. In the meantime, he was only pressing and rubbing his lips against mine slowly and sensually, and it was soft and wet, and also incredibly lust-inducing.

I couldn't help but start to feel some wetness in my pussy, which was only growing more soiled as time passed. In the meantime, it was as though the kiss was taking everything I had.

It was even stealing the breath from my lungs, something I

never thought would happen to me.

Then, he stopped the kiss, retreating his head slowly. "I'm not going to say I'm sorry about this, but I'm going to say that this isn't why I took you here."

I smiled, finding his words funny. I knew he had some humor in him, but I didn't think that it was actually so silly.

"And I never thought that tonight I was going to be kissing my own host," I murmured, and then I knew that everything else I was hiding from him - and there were still a couple of facts about me he had yet to learn – was finally going to come out.

Even though this was sudden and unexpected, I knew that it was the right thing to do.

CHAPTER 6

Curzio

Not thinking that I was going to be kissing Silvia, I couldn't help but start to miss her soft lips already. Her inexperience showed, but it wasn't like I expected any different. After all, it was more than obvious she was a virgin.

The gleam in her eyes was evident about what it was telling me, though. She wasn't going to say anything about that, and I couldn't care less. It wouldn't change anything, after all

Brushing my hand on her cheek, I said, "Now I know why you were crying, and I want you to know that you don't have to do that again as long as you have me." I took a deep breath in, wondering if I should reveal that side about me as well. Actually, though, it was a no-brainer. "I'm a Daddy – the kind of Daddy you are looking for."

She blinked twice, obviously not understanding me the first time I said it. Deciding that I wasn't going to squander this opportunity, I said, "And you don't need to have any doubts about it."

I brushed my index finger over her bottom lip, enjoying how smooth it was. She was plus size and, looking down, I realized it was something about her I loved. I couldn't help myself. Upon noticing that she wasn't opposed to it, I decided to do what most people would think was crazy.

I began to slide my hand over her curves and under her shirt, pulling it up and slowly. Silvia didn't even attempt to stop me, actually putting her arms up to help me.

I took a deep breath in, smelling her natural smell. There was something about it that was remarkably curious and lust-inducing, and it was at this moment that I felt my cock twitching in my pants. How I wanted to be inside of her right at this moment.

But she was a Little and I had to take my time with her. I wasn't going to do anything that could spook this stunning, jaw-dropping woman.

"I never thought you were," she replied. "I thought you were looking for someone more experienced, more 'normal'-"

And as soon as she said that, I pressed my finger against her lips, stopping her from continuing that line of thought. It was just wrong.

"Normal? You don't know what you're talking about. There's nothing wrong with you, and I want you to keep that in mind. I want you to remember that as you think about me," I murmured, giving her lips another peck and then one more for good measure.

"Daddy?" She asked and her voice was much more childish this time. It was like she was really slipping into the world of Littles right in front of my eyes, and knowing that was only making me harder.

It was impossible to control my erection.

I finished taking off her shirt and then tossed it to the other side of the room, where it wasn't going to bother us. Her torso was almost fully exposed, and it was as jaw-dropping as I thought. Looking at it, I couldn't help but start to massage her skin slowly and sensually with my fingers, enjoying every second of this.

"Thank you for saying that," Silvia said, putting her fingers under my shirt and feeling my muscles even as she did that, something that made my dick give a little somersault under my pair of boxer briefs. I knew that she could do some foreplay when she wanted, but I didn't think she could deliver her words so proficiently. The way she said them was hot, driving me to push her until she was lying on the bed and I was on top of her.

It was as though everything was happening in slow motion

around us.

I was with my arms on both sides of her, noticing how slow her breathing was. In the meantime, my fingers slithered over her curves, going around her and then removing her bra, finally revealing, for the delight of my eyes, how perfect her bosom was.

And noticing that, I pinched her nipples and started to play with them. Silvia turned her head, hissed, and then arched her back, almost rubbing her groin against me. Was that some kind of signal she was giving me? I didn't know, but it made me think about it, obsessing over the outcome of this, me penetrating her.

"How do you want me to do this, princess?" I asked, slithering my hands on the sides of her body and enjoying every part of it.

That was the question I asked, but I was certain she didn't have enough strength to say anything right now.

And she didn't. For the next few seconds, her mouth remained shut. In the meantime, I couldn't help myself, removing every piece of clothing we still had, and finally exposing, for the delight of her eyes, how I looked without my clothes on.

She reopened her eyes and, for the first few seconds, it was as though she thought she was dreaming. Then, she gasped when her mind finished processing what her eyes were witnessing. She had already drawn a sketch of my naked body in her mind, but it didn't hold a candle to the real thing.

"Daddy..." She cooed, throwing her legs around me and pushing me down so that our bodies were pressing against each other. I was still using my weight, my hands and arm supporting it, so that I didn't hurt her.

I could feel some saliva coming out of my mouth, wetting the sides of it. Her body was devoid of imperfections the way it was and I just wanted to keep feeling every part of it for as long as this lasted.

I went down, kissing her lips again and one more time, her body squirming and writhing under mine. Seeing her pussy for the first time, I couldn't help myself. I just had to do it, and I knew that Silvia was begging for me to start doing what I was.

I shot my hand to where it was, finding her clit and starting to rub it, my fingers fast and possessive, and her entire body resonating, following my rhythm.

"Oh God, oh God," she started to say, showing how different she was being right now from her usual self. I was overjoyed that she was feeling so much arousal. It was overflowing, her body turning slightly red, and her skin so wet that it was slippery.

I stopped brushing my finger on her clit, letting her catch her breath, and it worked. For the next few seconds, she reopened her eyes and they checked me out slowly from bottom to top. We were only gazing at each other as we asked several questions about how to finish this.

Silvia had just hit her orgasm and, after finding out how good it was, she wanted more. Except that this time, I was going to help her with that by doing something a little more drastic.

Not thinking again about it, I reached for the top drawer, opened it, and then picked up a condom. I ripped it out of the package, slid it on my cock, and finally penetrated her after putting her legs over my shoulders.

I began to roll my hips and my pace was slow in the beginning. It had the pace of a snail then, but a couple of seconds later, it picked up. I started to ram against her willing, begging core, and she was matching me thrust for thrust. It was everything I thought it was going to be, and a couple of seconds later, I finally reached my orgasm as well.

Silvia achieved her climax at the same time as I did, her eyes rolling inside her head, her toes curling. She held onto me as much as she could and when it was finally over, she collapsed on the bed. I fell onto the mattress as well and looped my arms around her, bringing her closer to me.

I had no idea what this meant, but if we could ever become much more than what we were to each other when we first met, I would be okay with it. This whole time, I just never thought she was a Little and now I knew she was.

I closed my eyes, falling asleep. What were the days from tomorrow onward going to bring us?

CHAPTER 7

Reopening my eyes, never before did I feel so light. Of course I was going to be feeling like this, I thought. Never before did I have a man with his arms around me, hugging me from behind, also snoring slightly. It wasn't loud or annoying, and it was actually comforting.

I didn't want to get out of bed, but the truth was that I had a couple of important things to do right now. I had to go back to my apartment, grab my things, and take them here. If it were up to me, I would be sleeping in this bed for hours on end, but things weren't so simple.

When I started to move my body slightly, Curzio groaned behind me, his fingers brushing over my bosom. I felt a crack of electricity traversing my body when his thumb scratched over my right nipple. Chances were that it hadn't been intentional, but it didn't matter and a moan escaped my lips, finishing waking him up.

"Silvia? You are already awake?" He asked, his breath hot and wet on my neck. "I didn't know you already were."

"I just woke up, actually," I replied and then he moved his arms away from me, annoying me somewhat. I wanted him to keep his arms around me for as long as he could.

This morning was one of the few where I felt safe and that nothing could ever hurt me. His arms around me only made that stronger.

"Then, you should get something to eat. I don't do this often, but I think I'm going to the kitchen myself and whip up something tasty for you."

My eyes went wide. I never thought that the owner of this jaw-dropping mansion, the man that stole my heart was going to do the cooking himself. I mean, someone that had so much money and was so powerful probably had a team of cooks working for him.

That was why I was finding his words surprising.

And Curzio didn't notice my reaction, sitting up on the bed. I could still feel the warmth of his body on me, and I wasn't ready to spend the next couple of seconds without it. It was for that reason, right at that moment, that I threw my arms around him, hugging him with vigor.

He looked down at me, smiling softly as he showed me his flawless teeth.

"Silvia, you don't need to be like this. I'm going to be gone for only a couple of minutes. I might not look like it, but when I'm in the mood, I'm a good cook."

I craned my head up, finding his eyes. They were different this time. Gentler, more comforting, and less threatening.

He brushed his hand over my forehead, pushing some of my hair to the side and putting it behind my ear.

I was going to miss him for the next few minutes, but he was my Daddy - or at least I thought he was – and I knew I was strong enough to be without him during that time.

He smiled again, slipping out of the bed and showing me how perfect his behind was. My eyes turned up and down, checking every part of it, wishing that my fingers were sliding over his asscheeks.

Then, he got dressed and walked out of the bedroom, leaving me alone. The worst thing about this was having to be thinking about everything that happened.

The positive was that I had found someone willing to put his life on the line for me. I could hear his footsteps walking down the hallway, reassuring me that this wasn't a dream.

I lied down on the bed again and continued to gaze at the ceiling, for the time being pushing away all the stray thoughts in my mind. It was more difficult than I thought it was going to be, but for now, I wasn't having another panic attack.

I closed my eyes and when I reopened them, Daddy was already coming inside the bedroom. He wasn't lying when he said he was going to whip up something for me, and the silver platter he was holding in his hands was showing me that.

The smell was already enough to stir my stomach, making me hear its rumbling in the silence of the bedroom. He sat on the edge of the bed and then smiled without showing his teeth, gazing at me with such comforting eyes.

"You look like a real princess sitting on the bed like this."

"Are we boyfriend and girlfriend already?" I asked and he widened his smile a little bit.

"We can be whatever you want, little princess," he said and then started to give me the food that was on the silver platter.

This was so romantic. He was giving me the food and I didn't even have to use my hands. Was I dreaming? This was like it was in my dreams, like when I thought I would finally have someone I could call my Daddy.

It wasn't a dream, I thought when I glanced down at the platter and noticed it was already empty. All that breakfast already gone? I asked myself, widening my eyes, looking stupefied. I knew I was hungry, but I didn't think it was so severe.

"Looks like someone hadn't eaten well in a very long time," he said and I wondered something, which I immediately asked him about.

"Wait, Daddy, aren't you going to eat anything?" I asked and he shook his head, standing up.

"I can't. I have something to do. I'm so sorry that my life looks so busy, but you don't need to worry about it. I'm going to make time for you when I can."

I remained where I was, for the time being unable to process what he just said. He wasn't going to have time for me right now?

A pity, but there was nothing I could do about it. I was just hoping that it wasn't going to become a tendency between us.

He brushed his hand on my forehead slowly, his eyes becoming gentler.

"I'm going to go out now, but you can explore the mansion. There's so much here you haven't seen yet," he murmured, turned, and left after taking a shower.

I wished I was with him in the shower box, I thought.

I remained where I was, checking my surroundings. I thought I was going to find something interesting, but for the time being, there was nothing.

Our bedroom – and it felt right to be saying that – was nothing more than that. Just another luxurious, rich bedroom, but still lacking anything out of the ordinary. Or at least, that was what I was thinking until my eyes stumbled on something that immediately drew their attention to them.

It was a small portrait, horizontal. It was on a small table on the other side of the room, which explained why it took me more than a couple of seconds to notice it.

But even when I did, my body felt lazy. I couldn't just get out of the bed, but I had to. With that thought in mind, I sighed, slid out of the bed, and started to pad over to the small table that supported the portrait.

I picked it up, scrutinizing it. It really showed Curzio and someone else that made my heart feel tight. The first thought that came into my mind was that she was Curzio's previous partner. Considering that he already had someone, then what was stopping him from realizing that I might possibly not be the person he was looking for to complete his life?

As soon as that thought crossed my mind, I put the portrait back down on the table. Thinking about that thing wasn't going to help me now. If there was something about me I wished to change one day, it was my paranoia.

I was always paranoid, especially when something good was happening in my life. Not thinking about it anymore, I turned around quickly and started to get dressed so that I could do the things he suggested I should.

After putting on a pair of soft shoes, I stepped out of the bedroom and started to explore the place – his mansion. It really was so much more than I thought it was.

And yet, it was also empty. Not empty in the sense that there weren't enough people around or that it didn't have many things to do here, but that it didn't have the only person I wanted to be with right now. Not to mention that I couldn't know much about my Daddy without talking to him face-to-face unless I wanted to do that behind his back. Not a chance I ever would, I affirmed.

I wasn't going to do anything behind the back of the only person that cared about me.

I did have some family, a father, and a mother, but they were nowhere I knew. Just thinking about them was enough to stir something hateful in me, and if there was something I didn't want to be feeling at the moment, it was that.

Thus, I just brushed those thoughts out of my mind and went down to the tennis court on the other side of the estate. I never played tennis before, but it was going to be good to learn how to now.

Not to mention that I could pass the time until Daddy came back and could hold me in his confident arms again.

CHAPTER 8

Curzio

I was alone at the dive bar and outside of it, resting my back on the wall, smoking my cigarette. The city was quiet. Other than the driving cars in the streets and some people perambulating here and there, one could even relax and have a good time here, despite the drug addicts, the criminals, and the rest of the scourge that ruined the city.

I was thinking about my Little and how much she was probably thinking about me at the moment. After all, I told her I was going to be back soon, but that was until I realized my day was so busy that I couldn't do that.

I called her and told her I was okay and that I was going to be back tonight, but glancing down at my wristwatch, I was already thinking I might have underestimated that as well.

It was almost midnight and her uncle hadn't come yet. I knew she told me the truth when she said he liked coming to this place, which was why I was hopeful I was going to find him here tonight - eventually.

I took another drag off my cigarette and tossed it on the ground, stepping and crushing it when I noticed someone coming this way, on the same sidewalk, his hands in his pockets and his head dipped. He was taking short, quick footsteps, and that face... I knew it even before he lifted it slightly.

He was indeed Silvia's uncle and was coming in my direction.

I had seen his face at the warehouse, but he hadn't seen mine. That was why I wasn't worried about hiding it. I looked like any man in his mid-thirties going to knock a few back, thus he had no reason to suspect I had come here for him.

Seconds later, he entered the bar, shutting the door behind him with an audible thump. He really was in a hurry, I thought, wondering if they served something else at the bar.

With my hands in my pockets, I entered the bar and closed the door gently. As soon as I was inside it, I noticed how empty it was. Only a few people were sitting at one of the far tables, chatting and laughing, not disturbing the peace. Other than that, the place was dead-silent, something that would be appeasing me right now if it wasn't for the fact that I hated this kind of place.

It just wasn't for me. Take me to a stylish, high-end pub located on the top of one of the skyscrapers, and I would have a blast.

This dive bar disgusted me, but I couldn't do anything about it. I noticed that Silvia's uncle, whose name she said was Alphonso, was sitting in front of the bartender.

She was most likely in her 40s, with ginger hair, wrinkles on her face, and in her hands, she was wiping clean a small glass. She glanced at me as soon as she noticed my arrival, eyes glaring.

Even though I looked the part, coming here looking like any other drunkard, she knew I was new here.

Not thinking about that, I made my way to the long table where Alpha was sitting. My feet made no sound, and in less than a couple of seconds, I was already sitting by his side.

"The usual, Alphonso?" The bartender asked and, in the first few seconds, Alphonso acted like he didn't hear it. I waited to see if that was going to change, but it didn't.

The bartender slapped the glass on the table, making him snap his head up.

"The usual, Alphonso? I asked you a question, but you didn't pay attention. Something worrying you?" She asked, and I wondered if he was going to say anything. It could give me more information about what he was doing here, perhaps even pointing to where Ausilio was. Now that I knew he was thinking about kidnapping Silvia, all I knew was that I was going to destroy him. Not just kill him, but crush him until nothing was left of him.

I felt this bubbling rage in my veins, remembering that Alphonso here was the one that made it all possible. He was the one that drugged Silvia, took her to that warehouse, and no matter what he said to me when I was alone with him, he would never be able to change my mind. His fate was already chosen.

I promised I wasn't going to hurt him, and I really wasn't. Still, I wished that Silvia wasn't so kindhearted.

"Nothing. Just give me the usual to drink. I need it."

"Are you going to pay this time?" The bartender asked, fisting her hands and putting them on her waist. "Because your tab is already too high and I'm getting tired of waiting for the payment."

He shook his shoulders as if he couldn't care less about that.

"I'm going to pay you tomorrow."

"Tomorrow? You sure about that?" She asked and I finally saw the opportunity I was looking for.

"I can pay his tab," I offered and he snapped his head to me, widening his eyes.

"Do I know you? Why do you want to pay my tab?"

"Let's just say that I'm new here in the city and that I want to make some friends." I had no idea if that was going to stick, but I was hopeful. Not to mention that nobody here would try anything against me and, if they did, I knew how to protect myself against a group of fewer than 10 assailants.

A moment of silence hung in the air and I wondered if he was going to take me up on my offer.

He shrugged his shoulders again, offering me his hand as he tried to smile. But his smile was ugly and stomach-churning. The moment he opened his mouth, I noticed his dirty, yellow teeth, finding out that he wasn't just addicted to heroin, but also crack.

No wonder he sacrificed his own sister just so that he could have a bit more money. In the end, it didn't work out for him, though.

Minutes later, after he knocked back a few, he looked much

more radiant and was even smiling. His gait was also filled with joy and he was following me as though I was his best friend.

"You are a good guy. I never thought there was anyone in this world with a heart as good as yours," he commented and when we were entering an alleyway, finally being alone, I slammed his body against the wall, shoving my arm up against his chest but without hurting him. Just like I promised Silvia, he was going to come out of this unscathed even though the police were going to lock him up.

"What the hell?" He shouted, but the moment he thought he was going to start to scream or beg for help, I shut his mouth with my hand. If he tried to bite it, I wouldn't hesitate before doing something much worse. And he knew that as soon as his eyes found mine.

"I know what you did."

When his breathing was calmer and I felt I could trust him to not beg for help, I retreated my hand and allowed him some space to talk.

He took a deep breath and then asked, "What did I do? I thought that we were beginning to understand each other, that you were a good guy."

"I'm not a good guy and I'm not trying to be one. I'm here because of Silvia, and I want to know everything you know about Ausilio. I know that he betrayed you and didn't give you the money he owed. I want to kill him. Even though I don't think about it this way, you can have your revenge if you help me."

His eyes studied my expression, realizing that I was telling him the truth. He took another long breath and then started to vent about everything that happened, including the fact that he was addicted to heroin and crack.

I could have felt some pity for him, but I didn't, I thought after my ears picked up the wail of the police sirens in the distance.

I knew that they were coming, which meant I had to make myself scarce. Not giving that another thought or consideration, I ran off, took the right, entered my car, and then turned on the engine.

It turned out that Alphonso didn't know everything about Ausilio - not everything I needed, anyway, but it was still enough for me to have some hope that I was going to find him.

And that, considering the current circumstances, was more than enough.

CHAPTER 9

Curzio

I took a deep breath in, wondering if I was going to be able to finally achieve my goal. I knew that the man I most despised was in the room inside the building across the street. I was with my sniper rifle perched on my shoulder, waiting for him to finally show up.

I knew he was going to. I knew that he would eventually cross in front of the window. He thought that nobody was looking, that nobody knew he was living there, but after a lot of digging and searching, I finally found out that he was hiding in that building.

It was a decrypt building on the outskirts of the city and just being at this place was dangerous. After all, someone that happened to know me could find out that I was here and come for my life. Few people knew who I was, and the ones that knew could take my life in less than a second. I wasn't saying that it was going to happen, just that I preferred doing this while everybody thought that I was safely tucked in my house, not doing anything.

For the time being, I wasn't thinking about that. The only thing I was thinking about right now, snow covering my shoulders, was how good I was going to feel when I finally killed the man that destroyed my life and made it a living hell.

It was cold, so cold that my bones shivered slightly, a gust of wind behind me making my teeth jitter. I didn't feel like spending another minute in this weather, but there was no denying that it was… kind of fitting for someone like me.

I thought that I could better control my feelings under any kind of pressure, but right now, even though I was doing my best to keep my aim focused on the small window, I could still feel it trembling slightly, and I was certain that it wasn't because of the chill of the air around me.

In the meantime, I couldn't help but think that this was anticlimactic. I'd always thought that I would kill him in person, plucking out his eyes while he was still alive, but that wasn't going to happen anymore.

Right now, I just couldn't stop thinking about the person that I still had so much to learn. This wasn't happening on the same night when I caused Alphonso to go to jail. It couldn't be, after all. Digging for information on Ausilio's whereabouts was difficult and a process that took a lot of time.

This was happening after that. Months after, and, during that time, I learned a lot about Silvia, what her life was like, what she was looking for in a man, and I couldn't wait until I was finally back home, putting her to sleep, checking if she obeyed all the rules, and overall having a blast with her.

It was all this was about, I thought, a sliver of joy surging in me when his head finally showed up right behind the window. It was just a flash of a moment that would have been ignored by most people – and even other hitmen - but I was different.

I was looking for this moment, for this opportunity, and when his head finally crossed the aim of the sniper rifle, I knew I had the solution that was going to end this torment.

It was a silenced shot and nobody other than me heard it. I wondered what he was thinking, hiding in that building, not even bothering to look out the window, even after the bullet pierced his head and I saw the blood blowing in different directions, tainting the walls of the small room where he was.

And then, nothing happened for the first few seconds. After all, he was alone in that room and it would take some time until his bodyguards noticed what happened. In the meantime, I could revel in what my eyes were seeing, and it was marvelous.

I finally turned my sniper rifle, resting it on my body before lying with it on my back. I could feel the coldness seeping into my bones, and it was a good reminder that my life, other than in the moments when I was with Silvia, would always be plagued by feelings and thoughts like that one.

I looked up, finding the sky and noticing how cold and grayish it was. When I noticed some buzz and confusion coming from down below and the building across the street, I knew that this was my cue.

My cue to finally leave and go back to my little one. I didn't need to look through the scope to know that my nemesis was finally dead. I knew he was, and that was the most comforting thing I ever felt.

I climbed down the building and found myself in the street, people still hurrying over to the building where Ausilio died. A hitman's kills were always like this. No fluff, no buzz, no commemorations, and the only thing that mattered was knowing that my target was finally dead.

Just thinking that was enough to make me feel so much better when I put my fingers on the steering wheel. I turned the car key, hearing the low rumbling of the engine, and then I started to drive over to the estate where I knew that my Little was going to be waiting for me.

I did check the news to make sure that people were going to report it as nothing more than another hit – and there were a lot of those happening around here, so it was nothing new.

I took a deep breath in, getting out of the car after realizing that I was going to have another blast with Silvia. She was already rushing out of the house to come and see me.

I opened a big smile, seeing that. Just couldn't wait to lift her in my arms.

SILVIA'S EPILOGUE

"**S**o, are you finally feeling better after killing him?" I asked, hoping that his accomplishment was going to give him some relief. After all, checking out the expression on his face, I knew how much of a toll this was taking on him.

Curzio was with his hands between his thighs, looking at me, and... he was actually smiling! I never thought he was going to be. I thought that taking the life of a man was either something he didn't feel anything about, being a hitman and all that, or was going to make him realize that it wasn't the solution he actually needed.

But that wasn't what he was showing me. His hand grabbed mine, holding it gently as he brushed his fingers on it.

"This is the best day of my life," Curzio confessed, making me remember that, when my uncle said he was a killer, he was right from the start even though I thought he was lying. I never thought that I would fall in love with a criminal, but it happened.

The things Curzio did... To the eyes of the justice system, he should be in jail alongside my uncle, but he wasn't and I would never do anything that might tip off the police about his crimes.

"And I love you so much," he said, in a blink putting his hands under my ass and lifting me, allowing me to wrap my legs around his waist. It was strong and muscly, and I could feel his muscles working as he walked around with me without a particular destination in mind.

I gasped. This wasn't the first time he was holding me like this and was doing this, but it was always surprising. Not to mention that I always fell a little bit more in love with him every time he did this, his fingers pressing into my butt.

When I recomposed myself, I told him, "And I love you too. You are the only person I want to spend the rest of my life with."

He was cold, though. I could feel that after putting my hands on his neck and kissing his lips. He was outside for an extended period of time, so it was expected. And yet, I still just wanted to lie down with him in our bed.

I'd been so nervous, thinking about what he had said before he left. He had told me he was going out alone. Even though he was a hitman and preferred achieving his goals on his own, I'd hoped that he would do the right thing and take his subordinates so that they could help him, but he didn't.

He turned on the TV after picking up the remote with a swift movement of his arm. He was looking at it and wanted me to see it as well. The reporter was showing that someone was murdered in that building and that, most likely, the shot had come from the building across the street, where my Daddy had been.

Were things always going to be like this? Was his life always going to be at risk? If that was the case, then it needed to be changed. With that thought in mind, I put my hand on his chin and made him turn his head, looking at me.

"Can we not think and talk about that anymore?" I asked and he quirked up his eyebrow, regarding me with some confusion in his eyes.

"Why? I thought you were going to be as happy about this as I am," he said after turning off the TV. I was content that he didn't feel worse about my words than I thought he was going to be. To be honest, checking his face, I could tell that he was taking my request well.

I took a deep breath when he opened the door to our bedroom. He put me on the bed slowly and gently, getting on one knee in front of me. I supposed that was his way of showing me he was putting himself in a more submissive position and exposing how much respect he had for me.

"I just want to live a life with you where I don't have to think and worry that someone is going to kill us," I murmured and he took a deep breath, glancing down at the floor.

"I've actually been thinking about that for a while now," he murmured, grabbing both of my hands so that he was holding them gently.

A moment of silence hung in the air and I wondered if he was going to tell me what I was waiting for the most. My heart was tight and beating like a galloping horse. It was the first time I was feeling like this, as though my world was going to explode if he didn't tell me what I wanted to hear.

"So, are you going to finally drop this and stop being a hitman?" I insisted, and he took another breath, sighing.

"I suppose that there's no helping it, so yeah, I'm going to do it, even though it goes against everything I told Adelmo about me. I always told him that I was going to lead the family, that I was going to make it much better than it is, and I never thought that I would see myself following in his footsteps again. If he looked at me now, he would probably be chuckling."

After hearing that, there was only one thing that needed to be done, and that was throwing my arms around him and over his nape, hugging him tightly. As if that wasn't enough, Curzio pushed himself against me and made me lie down on the bed with him.

I knew that we were going to make love, and I couldn't wait for it.

CURZIO'S EPILOGUE

"Everything's going to work out, I guarantee you," Adelmo said, smiling softly as he finished tying my tie. It was a black bowtie and I couldn't help but wonder why it was even necessary. It wasn't like it was going to make much of a difference, and I could feel the pressure it was applying on my neck, too. What a pesky little thing.

I didn't know if it was one of its 'attributes,' but whatever it was, it was annoying.

That had to be one of the reasons why Adelmo chuckled again. I didn't know why he thought he had to be the one to help me get dressed for the wedding. I supposed it was because he could see himself in me again. After all, he also fell in love with a Little.

I knew she was the one chatting with Silvia right now, most likely comforting her and showing her that everything was going to be okay. Adelmo told me that this wedding was going to be different, and I didn't believe him the first time he told me that.

From where I was, I could see part of the decoration in the chapel from across the garden, where it was going to take place. It was a little childish, pinkish, but fitting for the occasion.

People charged with finishing up the decoration hurried in and out of the building, looking sweaty and shouting sentences that I could hear even from where I was.

I glanced at Adelmo after he finished pulling inward the sides of the coat of the wedding suit, still smiling gently without showing his teeth. He felt proud of his 'work,' and it showed.

"Are you sure that everything is going to be okay?" I asked, checking the outside and growing more worried, still seeing too many people entering and leaving the chapel, running all around, shouting. What the hell was happening over there? I just hoped that the wedding was going to happen without an issue.

If it didn't, I wouldn't know what to do. After all, the wedding happening without major incidents was paramount to my happiness.

"I'm sure," he replied, putting his hand on my shoulder and then making me turn so that I could see myself in the mirror. I checked myself out in it with a glance, feeling so awkward. The truth was that this was the first time I was getting dressed for a social event of this caliber, and I didn't even know how I should be behaving properly.

The last thing I wanted was to see my Little looking at me and realizing that I wasn't the person she wanted to marry, even though that didn't make any sense. After all, she told me so many times how much she loved me, how much I was the one, and how important I was to her.

Just when I was going to turn around so that I was going to the chapel, they charged inside the room. The employees tasked to help me with getting dressed. They looked wide-eyed at me.

I brushed my hand, saying, "You're too late."

Everyone looked at me stupefied, wondering what was even going on right now. With wide, determined footsteps, I made my way down to the chapel. It was going to take some time, considering the distance, but it was nothing.

Finally. I was in the chapel a couple of seconds later, striding to the raised platform on the other side. I stood on it and then waited, looking for my Little, who was soon going to be showing up at the entrance.

When she was there, I knew I would barely be able to see her. The chapel was vast and the light coming from behind the entrance made it so I couldn't see much of what was actually happening outside.

It was okay, though. I didn't need to see my Little in detail from a distance.

Tapping my foot on the floor, I was already growing impatient. If there was something I learned in my life, it was that I didn't like to wait for anything.

Seconds later, Silvia finally showed up at the entrance and even though I couldn't see much more than a shadow, I knew she was stunning. I knew that her wedding dress looked like Snow White's, her jewelry gleaming and twinkling under the sunlight.

This was the best season of the year. The Summer was always exciting, especially given all the things we could do together. I was already planning on doing so many things with Silvia after the wedding night, which was going to take place outside of the country.

I was actually planning on moving out of here so that I didn't have to continue dealing with the bullshit that came with living in this place.

I took a long breath when she started to step down the aisle, her arm around the guy that was posing as her father. Her family disowned her a long time ago, and now the only real family she still had was me.

When the sunlight wasn't blocking her anymore, I could finally see how she looked, and she indeed did look just like Snow White. My hands were already prickling, my mind thinking about me putting the marriage ring on her finger and making my vows.

I was going to promise her I was going to give her the best life she could ever have, and she was going to do the same for me.

After all, I finally found my other half.

The End

Thank you and please leave your review. Your feedback helps me improve immensely!

TEASER: HIS PLUS SIZE LITTLE

Mafia Cupids - 1

The last thing I thought I was going to stumble on today was this menacing, frightening man that was lying on my bed. He was nothing short of jaw-dropping. Even though the clothes hid most of his body and he was unconscious, I could tell that he was those things and perhaps even much more than that.

He was just lying on my bed and even though I was helping him with his wounds, I had no idea what I was supposed to do right now. My hands were working. There was this hole in the side of his body, just under the rib cage, and even though it looked pretty bad, I knew that he was going to pull through.

To be honest, I was more frightened that he was going to wake up and find out how silly my room looked. The walls painted in pink, the stuffed toys spread around, and my teddy bear that was by the side of the bed – it also had something about a side of my life I always hid from other people, even the ones that considered me their friend.

I wiped the sweat that was on my forehead. I was a nurse – or at least I was going to be one again. They laid me off not too long ago and I was still living on the unemployment fund that they gave me. It was enough to pay the bills, but just barely so. My dingy little apartment was something that ashamed me, too.

Just looking at this hunk of a man lying on my bed, I was sure that he was someone used to richness and luxury, something that I never ever exposed myself to in my life. And yet, I was still going to keep helping him because, as a nurse, that's what I did.

Minutes later, I was finally finished patching up his wound. A lot of blood soaked the bedsheets and I could smell the blood in the air, but that was okay. It wasn't like I wasn't used to those things anyhow.

I was just so tired right now. This man was limping outside my bedroom when I noticed that he needed my help and that was when I went out of the room as quickly as possible. In a moment, I had found him still limping outside, and then he fell inside my room. I had gasped and it was a shock, but now not anymore.

I was already getting accustomed to the fact that this stranger, who was even carrying a gun with him, was in my apartment.

One other thing that was comforting me right now was the fact that he was still breathing, albeit slowly.

I couldn't help but wonder what he looked like without his clothes on. But that was a thought that I quickly brushed aside. There was no time to think about those things. It spoke about how lonely I always was, I thought, lamenting that part of my life.

Minutes later, when I was finally going to turn around on the little stool where I was sitting, I heard him grunting slightly and then he opened his eyes quickly. He found me and then he latched his hand on my wrist, something I thought he wasn't going to do.

After all, it was the first time that a patient was gripping my wrist so tightly after just waking up. His eyes were completely intense and glassy. He was looking at me with this intensity in his stare and I felt like he was going to kill me.

After all, even though he was slightly wounded, I was small and didn't know how to fight back against anyone. Even when a cockroach was hiding in the furniture and my eyes happened to catch sight of it, I always screamed at the top of my lungs like it was going to kill me.

Seconds later, though, the strange man eased his grip on my

wrist and he let his arm fall to the side of his body. He was still breathing slowly, and my heart rate was speeding up. He didn't say anything and it was infuriating. I didn't have to go out to help him and a thank you would be nice, I thought.

I turned around slowly so that my body was facing him. The man wasn't looking at me anymore, but rather at the ceiling and he was breathing slowly and carefully. I could see his chest expanding and contracting.

Moments later, when I was already opening my mouth so that we could begin to talk, he said, "Thank you for saving me. I would probably be dead right now if it wasn't for you."

I didn't even know what to say. I was so mad and so ready to dis him for not saying anything about my help, and now he just thanked me. I supposed that was why I was blushing and why he was chuckling when his eyes finally looked at me again.

But he didn't say anything about that, which was comforting and relieving.

"Well, I'm glad you are okay. I thought you were going to die," I said and then he didn't say anything else. There was this moment of silence between us, and it was awkward and I wanted to break it. "Are you going to tell me who you are?"

He stood up slowly, grimacing. It was obvious that the bullet wound still hurt him a lot and there wasn't much I could do about that, so he was just going to have to keep living with it for the time being. And me being the nurse I was, I had to do something he obviously didn't like.

So I put my hands on his shoulders and then I tried to make him lie down on the bed again, and he was already saying angrily, "Hey, I don't know what you think you're doing, but I'm okay. I feel better and I can stand up at least. Or if not that, I can sit on the bed."

"I'm not going to let you do that. I'm a nurse and I'm worried about you. You need to rest so that you can get better."

I was treating him like a child, but it was for a good reason. Even though there were so many mysteries surrounding his bullet wound, I was going to make sure that he was going to get out of my apartment feeling better and well.

He groaned slightly and was still strong enough to push back against my hands. I figured that this man was stubborn, but I didn't think it was this much and I also never thought he was still so strong. I mean, I was small and slightly chubby, but I thought I still had enough strength to push him back down.

When he was sitting on the bed, I just retreated my hands and then put them on my waist. I was shaking my head as I said, "I don't know what you think you are doing, but it's obviously not going to help you. I'm the nurse here and I'm the one that knows what I'm doing."

"I'm Adelmo Fiorentini, and it's good to meet you, nurse."

The way he said that made me blush. He was holding out his hand as if he truly cared that he was making my acquaintance. I didn't have another option but to give him my hand and I felt his fingers engulfing it like it was nothing. There was something about this man that gave me safety and pretty much everything else a Little like me could be looking for.

I knew that it didn't make sense, but what if he was a Daddy and was still single?

I shook that thought out of my mind right away. There was no point in believing in things that couldn't be.

His hand appeared to be holding mine for what felt like minutes, but when it was over, it was probably just a couple of seconds. His hand was particularly warm, big, and calloused.

It was the hand of a man that went through a lot before ending up where he was. His life was never easy, he was always facing the worst of things, and he had plenty of enemies.

Those were just some of my suppositions regarding his life and even though I knew that they were spot on, I wasn't going to just kick him out of the apartment. Not until he was feeling better. If I did something like that, I wouldn't feel okay with myself.

"And are you finally going to tell me your name?" He asked, raising his left eyebrow. Even though I didn't want to admit it, there was no denying that he was my type of man. There was just something about his face that made me want to kiss him, slide my hands on his cheeks, feel the bushiness of his beard, and do pretty much everything else I could.

Nevertheless, those things weren't going to happen right now. I was single and I was going to remain so for a long time.

I took a deep breath in and said, "I'm Dessie. Dessie Johnson."

SIMILAR BOOKS

SERIES - BIG ME

MM ABDL. Lots of age play, sweetness, peppered with steamy scenes, and sprinkled with age gap dynamics.

1. Pampering Little Miguel
2. Endless Crayons
3. Teaching Little Jerry

ABOUT THE AUTHOR

Amanda King writes sweet ABDL, age play romances. Packaged with steamy scenes, her books are fast-paced and, more often than not, they deeply explore the world of age gap relationships.

When she isn't writing, she's reading for inspiration. Some of her most popular stories are "Pampering Little Miguel" and "Endless Crayons."